For Ella and Amy – always follow your

dreams

xxx

Things with Wings

Rachael Phillips

Illustrated by Des Campbell

The magpie is a crafty bird that flies with black and white wings.

He really is a cheeky chap when stealing shiny things!

The moth can't see too well, when he flies in day or night.

He is so blind; he bumps a lot and even flies into lights!

The geese are very clever as they can float on water and fly.

They flock for miles, when it gets cold, in search of warm, blue sky!

The butterfly is the fairest of them all

and flies with delicate wings.

They drink the nectar from the flowers

and fly around colourful things!

The bat flies well at night and lives in caves beneath the ground.

They sleep up high, way off the floor by hanging upside down!

The robin is a friendly bird with a red breast
bold and bright.

His singing is heard all year round through
morning, noon and night!

The ladybird is black and red and covered with more than one spot.

It sleeps through winter, nice and snug and wakes up when it's hot!

The ostrich has wings but cannot fly

so is the funniest of them all.

It is the largest and fastest bird on land

and has a booming call!

The aeroplane flies way up high

and its engine spins and roars.

Children look up in wonder

as above the clouds it soars!

Things with wings are everywhere,

just take a look around.

When you spot a thing with wings

you'll be amazed at what you've found!

Coming soon in the *Things with...* series:

Things with Wheels

Things with Eyes

Things with Legs

You can find Rachael Phillips on

Facebook:

www.facebook.com/rachaelphillipsauthor

Twitter:

@rachfmphillips

Blog:

rachaelmphillips.blogspot.co.uk

You can find Des Campbell on

Blog:

threefingersorfour.blogspot.com

Printed in Great Britain
by Amazon.co.uk, Ltd.,
Marston Gate.